MANVILLE

THERE'S a BABY IN THERE!

by **Dandi Daley Mackall** ○ illustrated by **Carlynn Whitt**

A M A Z O N C H I L D R E N ' S
P U B L I S H I N G

Text copyright © 2012 by Dandi Daley Mackall
Illustrations copyright © 2012 by Carlynn Whitt

All rights reserved
Amazon Publishing
Attn: Amazon Children's Books
P.O. Box 400818
Las Vegas, NV 89149
www.amazon.com/amazonchildrenspublishing

Library of Congress Cataloging-in-Publication Data
Mackall, Dandi Daley.
There's a baby in there! / by Dandi Daley Mackall ; illustrated by Carlynn
Whitt. — 1st ed.
p. cm.
Summary: A four-year-old boy finds it hard to believe that a baby is
growing inside Mama's belly.
ISBN 978-0-7614-6191-3 (hardcover) — ISBN 978-0-7614-6193-7 (ebook)
[1. Babies—Fiction. 2. Brothers and sisters—Fiction.] I. Whitt, Carlynn,
ill. II. Title. III. Title: There is a baby in there!
PZ7.M1905Th 2012
[E]—dc23
2011034875

The illustrations are rendered in acrylic, colored pencil, and
wax crayon on watercolor paper.
Book design by Anahid Hamparian
Editor: Robin Benjamin

Printed in China (W)
First edition
10 9 8 7 6 5 4 3 2 1

For Ellie and Cassie Hendren,
who know all about being great siblings!
—D.D.M.

To Geoff, who believes in me
—C.W.

There's a baby in there.

At least that's what Mama and Papa tell me.
I don't think so.
I was in there once, four years ago. I didn't see anybody else.

I think I would've seen somebody if there had been
a baby in there.

Papa says, "No kidding! You're getting a
new playmate. There really is a baby in there."
That would be cool. . . .

But I still don't think there's a baby in there.

Granny comes over. She brings tiny
bananas tied in a pink bow and a
glow-in-the-dark gorilla night-light.
   "I'll be a monkey's uncle if this baby
doesn't turn out to be a girl!" Granny says.
"Yes, indeed. Your very own baby sister is
in there!"

Baby sister?

"Mama," I ask, "it's not a girl, is it? Couldn't you get a boy? An ape ball-playing boy, if you really do have a baby in there?"

Mama grins at me.

She puts my hands on her belly.

"Whoa!" Something in there kicked me.

What if there really is a baby in there?

"Papa, I've been thinking. If there really is a baby in there, won't it need a place to sleep when it comes out?"

"You're right!" Papa says. "It's time to build a nest for the baby."

Papa tries, but the new nest doesn't look very comfy.

"No more monkey business!" Granny shouts. "My grandson and I will fix this nest."

I help Granny bend branches and line the whole nest with soft leaves.

Then I put in my sock monkey.

My sock monkey will help that baby sleep, if there really is a baby in there.

"Granny," I ask at bath time, "I've been thinking. . . . If there really is a baby in there, doesn't the baby need a bath? There's not even room for a shower in there."

"A shower!" Granny says. "You're right. We need a baby shower."

It turns out a "baby shower" isn't a
real shower. It's a party where everyone
brings presents for the baby.

We unwrap rain forest rattles, a barrel
of monkeys, a King Kong crib, a monkeyshine
mirror, and a tiny jungle gym.

"Sorry the gifts are all for the baby," Mama says.

"That's okay," I tell her. "If there really is a baby

That night, Papa reads me a story, and I read him one.
"You're going to be a terrific big brother," he says.
If there really is a baby in there, I sure hope Papa's right.
"Come out, Baby, please?" Mama says.
"If there really is a baby in there," I whisper, "you better come out. Mama likes it when you do what she says."

Mama's eyes get big. "Oh. Oooooh.
Oooooh!"

"What?" I ask.

"This baby wants *out of there*! Go
get Granny!"

Papa and I do what Mama says.

Then we have to wait . . .
and wait. . . .

Guess what?

There *was* a baby in there!